The Nutty Nut Chase

Kathryn White
Illustrated by Vanessa Cabban

LITTLE TIGER PRESS
London

Hickory was making rude faces at Pecan when the strangest thing happened. A shiny, brown nut suddenly burst up from the ground. It wobbled and shook, then lay there, teasingly delicious.

"Wow, lunch!" Pecan shouted.

"Wow, lunch and dinner!" Hickory screeched.

POP!

"It's my nut," said Pecan.

"It's mine," snapped Hickory.

"Who's making that noise?" shouted
Badger. "I'm trying to sleep."

All the animals came out to see
what was happening.

"My nut!" Pecan shouted.

"It's mine!" yelled Hickory. "I saw it first."

"Box his ears!" shouted Littlest Rabbit.

"Certainly not. Boxing ears doesn't solve problems," said Badger firmly.

"Oh," said Littlest Rabbit, disappointed, "then bop his nose."

"No boxing or bopping," said Badger. "There will be a competition and the winner will get the nut."

"I know," said Hedgehog. "The prickliest wins the nut."

"But you're the prickliest," said Pecan.

"So I am!" said Hedgehog, delighted. "I win! I get the nut."

"Cuddliest gets the nut," said Littlest Rabbit. "I win!"

"ENOUGH!" said Badger. "We will have a race. First to reach the post wins."

"Hooray, a race!" everyone cheered.

Blackbird whistled the start
of the race. They were off.
Pecan and Hickory shot ahead
but the rabbits were close behind.
Hedgehog tried to run but only managed
a waddle. In a huff, he curled himself into
a ball and rolled full speed down the slope.

Littlest Rabbit looked back to see a
prickly ball spinning towards them.
"Look out!" he called.

Too late!

Hedgehog crashed through the racers like a cannonball and everyone landed in a prickly heap.

"Oh dear," tutted Badger. "We'll have to start again. And prickly cannonballs are not allowed."

Hedgehog snorted and sulked off.

Blackbird whistled and they were off again.
Pecan and Hickory were neck and neck.
 "My nut!" shouted Pecan triumphantly.
"I win!"
 "No!" shouted Hickory. "It's mine! I win!"

Suddenly the nut began to move.

It twitched and jerked, joggled and jiggled until PLOP! it disappeared down under the ground.

"It's a magic nut!" shouted Littlest Rabbit.

"Nutty magic!" squealed Hedgehog, racing back to see.

"I bet it would have tasted magic too," said Shrew.

POP!

The nut sprang up
right in front of Shrew.

"Quick, grab it!" shouted Littlest Rabbit.

All the animals shot across the grass,
rolling and shrieking, jumping and hopping,
banging and bopping into each other.

"I've got it!" shouted Hedgehog, but the
nut vanished again.
"That's my nose!" Shrew squeaked.

17

"Shhhhh!" said Badger suddenly. "Look."

He pointed at the magic nut that had appeared at his feet. Everyone tiptoed up to it. The nut shook and quivered. The animals looked in amazement.

"Help!" squealed the nut.

"AAAH!" shrieked Littlest Rabbit.
"A talking nut."

"You're a talking nut," said Pecan.

Heeelp!

Pecan and Hickory bent down and pulled and tugged, yanked and wrenched at the nut with all their might.

Out flew the nutshell, sending Pecan and Hickory rolling backwards. And there, where the nut had been, was Mole!

POP!

Mole shook himself and stood up on his two tiny legs. "Thanks!" he said. "I thought I would be stuck in that nutshell for ever."

Littlest Rabbit put the empty shell on his head. "It makes a great hat," he giggled.

"That looked like the tastiest nut ever," groaned Pecan and Hickory.

"There's plenty more where that came from," chirped Mole and he disappeared underground.

Suddenly shiny nuts began
popping up all over the place.
  "There's enough for everyone,"
Mole chuckled.

POP! POP!

"Magic!" shouted Hickory.
"Magic!" shouted Pecan.
"Nutty magic!" everyone shouted,
and they all munched with delight.

POP!

Picture Dictionary

Look at the words below and put the correct
picture stickers next to each word.

bird   butterfly

flower   nut

★ Have you got these right?
Then put a star on your reading tree!

 # Same Meanings

Match the words on the left to the words on the right that
have the same meaning. We've done the first one for you.

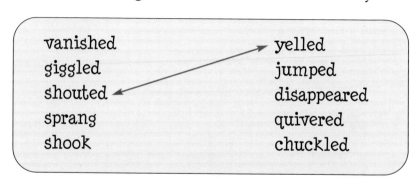

vanished   → yelled
giggled   jumped
shouted ←   disappeared
sprang   quivered
shook   chuckled

★ Did you match the words? Add another star to your reading tree.

 # Wonderful Word Search

Find the following ten words in the word search below.
The words can be found written down and across.

animals   huff   hat

magic   competition   quivered

grass   shell

hedgehog   shook

Y	S	H	O	O	K	F	O
C	J	E	P	M	L	X	Q
O	B	D	Q	D	S	H	U
M	A	G	I	C	W	A	I
P	N	E	V	Q	U	T	V
E	Z	H	U	F	F	A	E
T	F	O	D	I	T	K	R
I	L	G	R	A	S	S	E
T	F	X	O	Z	J	H	D
I	S	C	N	E	B	E	U
O	A	N	I	M	A	L	S
N	G	W	H	P	Y	L	K

Can you find these words in the story?

★ When you have done the word search,
add a star to your reading tree!

Drawing

Let's get creative! Draw a picture
in the frame for each word below.

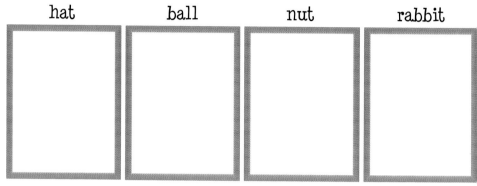

| hat | ball | nut | rabbit |

Did you find all these words in the story?

★ Did you draw all four pictures?
Add another star to your reading tree!

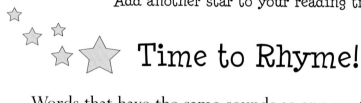

Time to Rhyme!

Words that have the same sounds as one another are called
rhyming words. E.g. grow – flow. Match them with their
rhyming words on the right.

1) brown	toes
2) mine	fox
3) face	nine
4) box	clown
5) nose	race

★ Did you get this right? Then add another star
to your reading tree!

 # Crazy Compound Words

When two short words join together,
they form a **compound word**.

Put the correct word stickers next to the words below to
make a compound word. Then write the new compound
word on the line. We've done the first one for you.

1) black   +   (bird)   =   **blackbird**

2) every   +   =   _____

3) nut   +   =   _____

4) cannon   +   =   _____

5) under   +   =   _____

Did you find these compound words in the story?

★ Did you get these right? Great!
Add another star to your reading tree.

 # Rhythmic Syllables

Every word is made up of one or more **syllables**. A word that is one beat long has one syllable, like "nut". A word that is two beats long, has two syllables, like "dinner" (din+ner). A word that is three beats long has three syllables, like "delicious" (de+li+cious).

Read out the words below. Count the syllables in each word and put the sticker with the correct number of syllables next to each word.

1) up   (1 syllable)
----

2) animal
----

3) badger
----

4) bop
----

5) empty
----

6) delighted

Did you find all these words in the story?

★ Have you got the syllables right?
Add the last star to your reading tree! Well done!